Little Genie
Castle Magic

Little Genie
Castle Magic

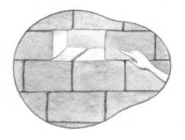

MIRANDA JONES

illustrated by David Calver

Delacorte Press

Published by
Delacorte Press
an imprint of
Random House Children's Books
a division of Random House, Inc.
New York

A Working Partners Book

Visit us on the Web! www.randomhouse.com/kids
Educators and librarians, for a variety of teaching tools, visit us at
www.randomhouse.com/teachers

Library of Congress Cataloging-in-Publication Data
Jones, Miranda.
Castle Magic / by Miranda Jones ; illustrated by David Calver.
p. cm. — (Little Genie)
"A Working Partners Book."
Summary: When Ali brings Little Genie along on a class trip
to a local castle, chaos ensues.
ISBN 0-385-73165-5 (trade) — ISBN 0-385-90203-4 (lib. bdg.)
[1. Genies—Fiction. 2. Magic—Fiction. 3. Wishes—Fiction.
4. School field trips—Fiction. 5. Castles—Fiction.]
I. Calver, David, ill. II. Title.
PZ7.J7237Cas 2004
[Fic]—dc22
2003018349

Printed in the United States of America

September 2004

10 9 8 7 6 5 4 3 2

BVG

Special thanks to Narinder Dhami

Don't miss these great books!

Little Genie

Contents

Chapter One
Absolutely No Way

October 3

How to Plan a School Trip
By Allison Katherine Miller

Yay! Today the whole fourth grade is going on a trip to a Real Live Castle! Of course, we don't get many castles in Cocoa Beach, but apparently this one was shipped over from Europe stone by stone when the owner moved here. It must have been like doing the biggest jigsaw puzzle in the world, fitting all the pieces back together again. I wonder if there were any pieces missing at the end, like there usually are when I do a puzzle. I'll have to tell Mary to look out for holes in the walls!

Anyway, Mrs. Jasmine says we have to do a project on castles by next week, so I'm going to make sure I get lots of notes and draw loads of pictures. Dad got a book on knights out of the library for me, and it's actually really interesting.

I don't want anything to go wrong today, so that means Genie can't come. It's not that I don't think she's the coolest thing ever; it's just that wherever she goes, trouble sure follows. I hate to think what she might do in a castle with all her goofy magic. So that's that. No Little Genie on the school trip.

Absolutely no way.

Chapter Two
One Hundred Pop Bottles

"Now, have I got everything?" Ali Miller said, peering inside her backpack. "Pens, pencils, sketchbook, purse, packed lunch . . ."

"I know something you've forgotten," Little Genie announced. She was standing on the edge of Ali's desk, a tiny, sparkling figure in her wide swirly-patterned pink pants, tight-fitting top, and golden slippers with curled-up toes.

Ali frowned. "What?"

"Me!" Genie danced up and down, her blond ponytail bobbing. "Please, can I come with you, Ali? Please, please, please!"

"Oh, Genie!" Ali sighed. "I thought we decided you were going to stay home."

Ever since Little Genie had popped out of a Lava lamp Ali's gran had bought for her, Ali's life had been turned upside down. Ali loved having a real, live genie. How many other people got to have three wishes granted by their very own magic friend? The only trouble was, Little Genie had missed so many lessons at Genie School that her magic was always mixed up!

"Listen, Genie," Ali said firmly. "I've been looking forward to this trip to

Baron Popplehoff's castle for ages. I don't want anything to go wrong!"

"I'll be really good," Little Genie promised, clasping her hands and gazing up at Ali with her huge blue eyes. "I'll be so good, you won't even know I'm there. I've never caused you a *big* problem, have I?"

Ali put her hands on her hips. "What about the tidal wave inside my school?" she reminded Genie. "And the pepper-flavored cookies? What about the bright pink soccer jerseys?"

"Oh, nothing like that will happen today," Genie said confidently. "Look, you won't even *have* any wishes." She held out her wrist with the tiny hourglass-shaped gold watch on it. Whenever the sparkling pink sand began running through the hourglass, Ali received three new wishes. The wishes lasted as long as it took for all the sand to run through, but because the hourglass worked on unpredictable genie time, neither Ali nor Genie ever knew how long that would be.

Ali stared at the hourglass. The top half was filled with pink sand and the bottom half was empty. "It's been two weeks since the last lot of wishes," she pointed out. "The sand might start running again today."

"I'm sure it won't!" Genie said. "And even if it does," she added solemnly, "I promise I won't do any magic unless you ask me to."

"Sorry, Genie." Ali sat down on her

bed and opened her flower change purse to see how much money she had. "I think it would be better if you stayed at home—oh!"

Ali almost jumped out of her skin as a puff of glittering pink smoke suddenly appeared right next to her. "Genie!" she gasped. "Was that you?" Coughing, she waved her hand in front of her face.

When the smoke cleared, Ali was amazed to see a huge wooden shield with a golden lion painted in the middle of it propped up against her backpack. "Wh-what's this?" she spluttered.

"Don't go ape!" Genie scolded. She was always using expressions from the sixties. Ali bet her gran would like talking to Genie.

"But what is it?" Ali asked.

"It's a shield," Genie announced happily. "I read about them in your history book." She pointed to a book lying on the desk next to her. The book was nearly as big as she was.

Ali tried to lift the shield. It was so

heavy she couldn't even move it. "I thought you said you weren't going to do any magic unless I asked you to," she said crossly. "And it's squashing my lunch!"

Genie wasn't listening. She had heaved the book open and was flipping through it. "You need a sword, too," she said. "Knights always carried a sword *and* a shield."

"No!" Ali said quickly as Genie closed her eyes and began to murmur a spell. "No sword! And get rid of the shield before my mom sees it."

Genie opened her eyes. "Are you sure?" she said. "Mrs. Jasmine might give you extra credit if you turn up with some real weapons."

"Quite sure," Ali said firmly.

Genie shrugged and sent the shield away with a puff of smoke. "There, all gone. So does that mean I can come with you?" she asked eagerly.

Ali rubbed her hand over her eyes. Little Genie was beginning to wear her out! "Wouldn't you rather stay here?" she pleaded.

Genie looked miserable. Her ponytail sagged. "But I always have to stay at home when you go to school."

"Can't you play with Marmalade?" Ali asked. Marmalade was the ginger cat that lived next door. He and Genie had been great friends ever since she had helped him scare away the bullying cats in the neighborhood that kept coming into his yard.

Genie shook her head. "No, he's going to the vet for his checkup this morning. I'll be *so-o-o-o* bored! Please let me come with you, Ali."

Ali frowned. If Little Genie was left on her own all day, she might get into even more mischief. Maybe it would be better if she *did* come on the trip to the castle after all. At least then Ali would be able to keep an eye on her!

"Okay . . . ," she began.

"Fantastic!" Little Genie shouted. And she turned three somersaults in the air, one after the other.

"But," Ali went on sternly, "*no* magic. Agreed?"

"Definitely no magic!" Little Genie opened her eyes very wide and put one hand over her heart. "I promise. I'll even stay lamp size all day so no one will see me." Sometimes Genie made herself full size, so that she was as tall as Ali, but Ali had to admit it was a lot easier to keep Genie hidden when she was the right size to fit into her Lava lamp home.

Ali lifted her backpack onto the desk and Genie jumped into the pocket. She snuggled down and waved up at Ali. "Don't worry," she called. "We're going to have a great time!"

"I hope so," Ali replied. She had just fastened the backpack pocket when she heard her mom calling up the stairs.

"Ali, are you ready? It's time to go."

"Coming," Ali called back. Carefully she

slung her backpack over her shoulder and ran downstairs.

"Have a good time!" Mr. Miller called from the kitchen.

"Yeah, and bring me back a sword!" added Ali's little brother, Jake, through a mouthful of Frosty Flakes.

Ha! Ali thought, imagining Bulldozer (as she liked to call him) with a sword. *No way!*

Her mom was waiting by the front door, car keys in her hand. "Are you looking forward to the trip?" she asked Ali as they went out to the car.

"Yes, I can't wait!" Ali said eagerly.

A tiny voice from inside the backpack pocket whispered, *"Neither can I!"*

∗   ∗   ∗

"Oh, look, Mom!" Ali said as Mrs. Miller pulled the car up outside the school. "The bus is already here."

"And there's Mary," her mom said. Mary Connolly was Ali's best friend. She was standing in the playground waving at them. "Off you go, then. Have a great time!"

"I will!" Ali said. She jumped out of the car clutching her backpack and hurried over to Mary. The rest of their class was already there, waiting to board the bus.

"Hi!" Mary greeted Ali. "I thought you weren't coming. You're the last one to get here."

"Sorry," Ali said. "I—um—couldn't find my sneakers." She couldn't tell Mary that Little Genie had made her late by popping the shield into her bedroom. Mary didn't know about Genie. In fact, Genie had told Ali that if she breathed a word to anyone about her new friend and her magic powers, Genie would have to go back into her Lava lamp forever and there would be no more wishes.

Just then Mrs. Jasmine hurried over, carrying a clipboard. "There you are, Ali," she said. "I was beginning to wonder where you were." She checked Ali's name off the list and then turned to the rest of the class. "We can get on the bus now," Mrs. Jasmine told everyone.

"Let's try to get the backseat," Ali said to Mary. "It's the best place to sit."

But as soon as the bus driver opened

the door, Tiffany Andrews pushed her way forward, along with her friends Sara Parker and Melanie Bell. "Mrs. Jasmine, I have to sit at the back of the bus," Tiffany announced loudly. "Otherwise I get carsick." Smirking and looking important, she marched to the front of the line and climbed onto the bus, followed by Sara and Melanie.

"Typical Tiffany!" Ali grumbled. "She always gets what she wants."

"Well, it's quieter for us if she does." Mary grinned at Ali. "I don't mind where we sit, as long as we're nowhere near Barry Jones!"

Ali and Mary found a seat and Ali carefully put her backpack on the floor. Unfortunately, Barry Jones sat down behind them, banging his backpack against Mary's head as he squeezed in.

"Ow!" Mary complained, rubbing her head.

"Sorry," Barry said. "Hey, this castle stuff is great!" he declared. "I'd love to have been a knight. I bet I'd be great at sword fighting!" He began slashing at the air with an imaginary sword and nearly hit Ali.

Ali sighed. Sometimes Barry Jones was as annoying as Jake—but Jake was only six, and Barry was nine, like Ali. She was beginning to wonder if she'd enjoy this trip at all with both Barry and Genie around to cause trouble!

There was a cheer as the bus driver started up the engine and pulled out of the parking lot at last.

"One hundred bottles of Popplehoff on the wall." Behind them Barry Jones launched into song. "One hundred bottles of pop. And if one pop bottle should happen to fall, there'll be ninety-nine bottles of pop on the wall!"

Mary groaned. "I hope he's not going to sing all the way to the castle."

"Well, he's still got ninety-nine bottles to go!" Ali pointed out.

Mary turned around and knelt on her seat to glare at Barry. "Are you going to sing for the whole trip?"

"I'm bored!" he complained.

"But we only just left the school playground!" Mary protested. "How can you be bored already?"

Ali smiled. Just then she felt something

tugging at the leg of her jeans. She looked down at the backpack. She could see Genie's arm poking out.

Ali glanced sideways to be sure that Mary was still arguing with Barry; then she bent over and undid the pocket. "What's the matter?" she whispered as Genie's blond head popped up.

"It's the hourglass," Genie whispered back. "The sand's started running through it." Genie's eyes grew wide. "Your wishes have started again!"

Chapter Three
Welcome to
Popplehoff Castle

"Oh no!" Ali bent lower to stare at the tiny watch on Genie's wrist. Sure enough, the pink sand had started slipping through the hourglass.

"Don't look so worried." Genie beamed at Ali. "You know how much you love having your wishes!"

Ali groaned quietly. It wasn't that she didn't *like* having three wishes. She'd loved looking after the cute cartoon tiger with purple fur that Genie had brought to life from a chocolate ad, for instance. But today she just wanted to enjoy the trip without worrying about magic spells going wrong.

"I'm not going to use *any* wishes while we're at Popplehoff Castle!" Ali said in a determined voice.

Genie looked very disappointed. "But if you wait until the trip is over, the sand might have run all through the hourglass by then," she pointed out. "Then you won't get any wishes at all."

"I'll just have to take that chance," Ali said. "No wishes and no magic!"

"Are you talking to yourself again?" Mary teased, turning around and settling back in her seat. Luckily, she seemed to have persuaded Barry to stop singing.

Ali blushed. "Um—no." She glanced down at the backpack and was relieved to see that Genie had popped out of sight again.

"Want a mint?" Barry leaned between the two seats and thrust a bag of peppermints at them. Ali had to jerk backward to stop Barry's finger from poking into her eye.

"Okay, thanks," she said. Maybe if Barry was eating candy, he wouldn't start singing again.

Barry yanked hard at the bag, trying to open it. Suddenly the bag split and Ali and Mary were showered with peppermints!

"Help!" Ali yelped as one hit her on the ear.

"Oops," Barry said. "Sorry."

"There isn't a single one left in the bag!" Mary said as she picked peppermints off her seat. "Honestly, Barry, can't you be more careful? And they aren't wrapped, so we can't eat them."

Ali bent over to collect some peppermints that had fallen on the floor in front of her. She was just in time to see Genie pop out of the pocket and snatch up a peppermint that had landed on the backpack.

Ali pushed the rest into the other backpack pocket and fastened it firmly. There was no point in giving them back to Barry now that they'd been all over the floor.

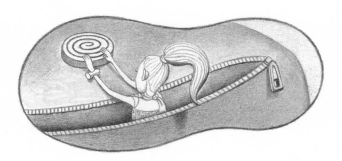

Barry slumped down in his seat with a sigh, looking dismally at the empty bag in his hand. A moment later, Ali and Mary heard "Eighty-nine bottles of Popplehoff on the wall" from the seat behind them.

Mary stuck her fingers in her ears and closed her eyes. "Tell me when we get there!" she moaned to Ali.

Ali laughed, then noticed Genie popping out of the backpack pocket again. She was licking her lips. *Surely she couldn't have eaten that peppermint already?* Ali thought. It was nearly as big as her head!

Genie glanced cautiously at Mary, who still had her eyes closed. She pointed over Ali's head at Barry and began waving her arms around. Then she put her hands over her ears and pulled a face. Ali grinned. Genie wasn't impressed by Barry Jones's singing either.

"Want me to stop him with a bit of magic?" Genie whispered to Ali.

"No!" Ali whispered back, alarmed. "Don't you dare!"

"Please!" Genie begged.

"No!" Ali said through clenched teeth.

Looking disappointed, Genie slipped down into the pocket again. This time Ali zipped it up. Barry was being really annoying with his endless songs and flying peppermints, but she'd rather put up with them than let Genie loose with her magic.

A little while later, when Barry was down to thirty-four bottles, Ali sat up in her seat and nudged Mary. "Look," she said excitedly. "Popplehoff Castle!"

The bus had turned down a long, sweeping driveway lined with leafy trees. Ahead of them stood a huge castle built of gray stone. At each of the four corners, turreted towers stretched up into the blue sky.

"It looks just like a castle *should* look!" Ali gasped. "Isn't it cool?"

"Let me see!" squeaked an excited voice from inside the backpack.

Ali looked flustered as Mary glanced around, puzzled. "Oh! I just wanted to see out the window on the other side of the bus," Ali said quickly, peering past her friend.

The bus rolled into the parking lot beside the castle and drew to a halt.

"Stay in your seats for a moment, please," Mrs. Jasmine called.

"Mrs. Jasmine, I need to get off the bus first," Tiffany Andrews announced from the backseat. "I feel sick."

Ali rolled her eyes at Mary. That was just like Tiffany—she had to be first to do *everything*!

Mrs. Jasmine looked suspicious. "I thought you said you were all right if you sat in the backseat," she reminded Tiffany.

"I am, usually," Tiffany sniffed. "But it was a really bumpy journey."

Ali and Mary grinned as the bus driver turned around to raise an eyebrow at Tiffany.

"Well, we'll all be getting off in just a few minutes," Mrs. Jasmine told her. "Please make sure you have your pencils and notebooks ready to take notes for your project. We're going to be shown around the castle by Mrs. Ledbetter, one of the official guides." Mrs. Jasmine pointed out the windows at a white-haired woman in a tweed suit and sensible shoes.

"Now," Mrs. Jasmine went on, "there are lots of valuable pictures and furniture in the castle, so make sure you don't touch anything unless you're told you can. I expect you all to be on your best behavior."

And that's why there won't be any wishes or any genie magic! Ali thought.

The driver opened the doors, and everyone grabbed their bags and followed Mrs. Jasmine off the bus.

"Welcome to Popplehoff Castle." Mrs. Ledbetter strode briskly forward and beamed at them. "It's very nice to meet you. Now, we have a lot to see, so will you please follow me?"

"She has a British accent!" Ali said.

"Maybe she came over with the castle!" Mary whispered back.

Everyone crowded around the guide as she ushered them through the huge archway. She told them that the first Baron Popplehoff had built Popplehoff Castle in Europe six hundred years ago.

"The present-day Baron Popplehoff and his family liked living in the castle so much, they decided to bring it with them when they moved to Cocoa Beach twenty years ago," Mrs. Ledbetter added.

"That's kind of weird, isn't it?" Mary remarked to Ali. "Having people walking around looking at your house while you're still living in it!"

Mrs. Ledbetter overheard her. "The

baron's living quarters are private," she explained. "We'll just be visiting those parts of the castle that are open to the public."

Ali felt something poke her in the shoulder. It was Genie, nudging her from inside the backpack. Ali moved away from the rest of the class and opened the pocket. Genie's head popped out.

"What's the matter?" Ali whispered.

"Can you leave the pocket open now?" Genie whispered back. "I want to see the castle."

"Well, okay," Ali agreed reluctantly. "But remember, no magic!"

"I promise," Genie said.

Ali slung the backpack back onto her shoulder and hurried to catch up with her class as they walked into the cobbled courtyard.

"Isn't this great?" Mary said, gazing around. "It's like traveling back in time."

Ali nodded. "Yeah, you can just imagine knights in armor and ladies in long flowing dresses walking around, can't you?"

"We'll start with the famous Green Bedroom in the West Tower," announced Mrs. Ledbetter. She led them over to one of the towers, and they began to climb the steep spiral staircase. "Many princes and princesses are supposed to have stayed in this room when visiting the Popplehoff family."

"Wow!" Ali breathed when she reached the top of the stairs and squeezed into the bedroom with the rest of the class. A vast four-poster bed stood in the middle, surrounded by pale green silk curtains. The furniture was cream and gold, and there were huge pictures in gilt frames on the walls. "It's fantastic!"

"What's in those glass cases over there?" Tiffany asked, pointing across the room. She bent down to duck under the rope that separated them from the main part of the room.

"Come *this* way, please," Mrs. Ledbetter said, giving Tiffany a stern look. She shepherded them around the roped-off section to the other side of the room where the glass cases were.

Ali was fascinated to see that they were filled with china dolls of all shapes and sizes. They were dressed in

old-fashioned outfits with long dresses, petticoats, and frilly bloomers.

"This is the world-famous Popplehoff collection of antique dolls," Mrs. Ledbetter told them.

"They're really nice," Ali said to Mary. "But I couldn't imagine playing with dolls that cost so much money!"

"Excuse me!" Tiffany said rudely,

elbowing Ali out of the way. "Do you mind if someone else takes a look?"

Ali rolled her eyes and shuffled sideways. It wasn't worth arguing with Tiffany.

"Look, Tiff," Sara Parker said. "That one in the pink dress looks like *your* antique doll."

Tiffany peered into the glass case. "Oh, yes," she agreed. "But mine's a lot nicer than that. Mine must be worth *loads* of money!"

"Ali!"

Ali jumped as she heard Little Genie's voice. Quickly she moved away from the rest of her group before anyone else could hear.

"Can I get out of the backpack and have a look at the dolls?" Genie asked.

"No!" Ali whispered firmly. "What if someone sees you?"

"I'll just keep really still," Genie told her. "They'll think I'm one of the dolls!"

Ali groaned. "For one thing, the dolls are in a glass case. And none of them are wearing bright pink pants! You won't exactly blend in."

"Let's go out into the corridor," Mrs. Ledbetter called, leading the way out of the bedroom.

"It's not fair," Genie grumbled from her pocket as Ali hung back to let the rest of the class leave the room. "I can't see very much from in here."

"Shhh!" Ali whispered. She was beginning to think it had been a very bad idea to bring Little Genie along.

The wood-paneled corridor was long and wide. Suits of silver armor were lined up along the walls from one end to the other. Ali thought suits of armor looked a bit scary. Someone could hide inside one of them, she thought, and you wouldn't even know they were there.

Mrs. Ledbetter was pointing out the large and colorful tapestries hanging on the walls. Some of them showed scenes of battles, while others had elaborate patterns of leaves and flowers. "Tapestries were often hung up to try to stop the chilly drafts," the guide explained. "Castles didn't have central heating, you know!"

Ali was standing at the back of the group listening to the guide when suddenly she noticed Barry Jones out of the corner of her eye. He was trying to pull one of the metal hands off a suit of armor.

"What are you doing?" Ali said in a low voice. "Mrs. Jasmine told you not to touch anything."

"I just wanted to try the hand on," Barry mumbled, glancing over his shoulder to make sure Mrs. Jasmine wasn't watching. "I wish I could try the whole suit!"

"I wish you could too," Ali said crossly. "It might keep you from annoying me for a minute!"

The second she said the words, Ali could have kicked herself. But it was too late. Way too late. Barry Jones had disappeared in a puff of glittering silvery smoke!

Chapter Four
Knight in Hiding Armor

"Barry!" Ali gasped. "Where are you?"

"In here!" said a muffled voice.

Ali bit her lip. She'd wished Barry Jones inside the suit of armor!

"That worked well, didn't it?" Genie popped up out of the pocket and beamed at Ali. "Maybe that'll keep Barry quiet."

"But I didn't mean to make a wish!" Ali groaned.

"How did I get in here?" Barry asked in

a puzzled voice. "Did you do something, Ali?"

"Never mind that," Ali said. Quickly she looked around. The class was following Mrs. Ledbetter down the corridor. "Just get out of there as fast as you can."

There were a few clanks as Barry tried to lift his hands inside the suit of armor. "I can't," he said at last. "It's too heavy!"

"What?" Ali exclaimed. "Let me try." She grasped one of the metal hand pieces and tried to pull it off. But she couldn't move it. Ali frowned. What was she going to do? She couldn't unwish the wish, unfortunately; it didn't work that way. She would have to wait for all the sand to run through the hourglass before Barry was free again.

"Don't worry, Ali," Genie said cheerfully, hanging out of the backpack pocket. "I think the armor really suits him."

"How can you tell?" Ali said. "You can't even see him!"

Genie grinned. "Exactly!"

"Ali!"

Genie ducked out of sight and Ali jumped. Mary was coming toward them.

"Come on!" she called. "Mrs. Ledbetter's taking us to see the kitchen."

"What about me?" Barry said from inside the suit of armor.

Mary almost leapt out of her skin. "That—that suit of armor just spoke to me!" she spluttered.

Ali heard a tiny chuckle from inside the

backpack. "It's Barry Jones," she told Mary. "He's inside it."

"Oh, honestly!" Mary exclaimed. "That's just the kind of stupid thing he *would* do!"

"Hey, I heard that!" Barry called out. "It wasn't my fault. *I* don't know how I got in here."

"He's stuck," Ali explained quickly before Mary could start asking questions about exactly how Barry *had* got into the armor. "What are we going to do? If Mrs. Jasmine or Mrs. Ledbetter finds out, there'll be big trouble." And Barry would be in big trouble too, Ali thought guiltily.

"You've got that right," Mary agreed with a frown. "Mrs. Jasmine might make us leave before we've seen the rest of the castle."

"We'll just have to try to make sure she doesn't find out," said Ali. She crossed her fingers behind her back, hoping that all the sand would have run through the hourglass by the time they went home. "Maybe Barry will find a way out of there by the time we leave," she suggested weakly.

"I hope so." Mary grinned. "I think Mrs. Jasmine might notice if there's a suit of armor sitting on the bus!"

"Barry, listen to me," Ali said, standing on tiptoe so that she could speak into the helmet. "You're going to have to come with us. But if Mrs. Jasmine or Mrs. Ledbetter or anyone from our class sees you, you'll have to stand really still and pretend you're one of the displays. Okay?"

"All right, but I don't know how easy it's going to be to walk around," Barry grumbled. "This armor's really heavy."

Ali and Mary watched anxiously as Barry began to move his arms and legs inside the metal suit.

"We'd better hurry," Mary warned. "The others have already gone downstairs."

With a good deal of huffing and puffing and creaking, Barry began to clank down the corridor toward the stairs. Ali and Mary followed on either side.

"I don't think I can get down the stairs," Barry said worriedly. "My legs won't bend!"

"We'll give you a hand," Ali told Barry.

She and Mary each took one of Barry's metal arms. He shuffled to the edge of the step and lurched down to the next one with Ali and Mary holding on to him tightly.

By the time they got halfway down, Ali's arms were beginning to ache. The suit of armor really was heavy. But it was her fault that Barry was stuck in there, so she couldn't leave him behind. At last they made it to the bottom of the staircase, where they could hear Mrs. Ledbetter's voice farther down the corridor.

"This painting is over three hundred years old," she was saying. "It shows Popplehoff Castle in the eighteenth century."

"Wait here for a minute, Barry," Ali

whispered. "You'll have to follow us as quietly as you can. But keep well back from the rest of the class."

"Okay." Barry tried to give Ali a thumbs-up, but he couldn't lift his arm very far.

"Now we'll go to the kitchen," Mrs. Ledbetter announced. "We have refurbished it to look as it would have two hundred years ago."

Ali and Mary hurried down the corridor to catch up with the rest of the group. Suddenly there was a loud *clang* from behind them.

"What was that?" Mrs. Ledbetter exclaimed.

Ali's heart began to thump as everyone turned around to look. But to her relief, Barry was standing against the wall, as still as stone. He looked just like one of the empty suits of armor!

"I think he just bumped into that table," Mary whispered in Ali's ear. "I don't suppose he can see very well with a helmet on."

Ali glanced anxiously over her shoulder as they went toward the kitchen. Barry was lumbering along behind them again, keeping a good distance between himself and the rest of the class.

The kitchen was enormous, with a high wood-beamed ceiling. An ancient wooden dresser with shelves full of heavy white crockery stood against one wall, and a log fire crackled in the hearth.

"We'd better help Barry," Ali whispered to Mary. "There are too many things in here for him to crash into!"

As Mrs. Ledbetter began to explain what kind of food the Popplehoffs would have eaten hundreds of years ago, Ali and Mary helped Barry into the room.

"Let's put him in the corner by the fireplace," Mary said in a low voice. "He'll be out of the way there."

"Hey, it's really hot here!" Barry complained as Ali and Mary shuffled him into position.

"Shhh!" Ali told him. "It's only for a few minutes."

Leaving Barry by the fire, Ali and Mary quickly rejoined the group.

"And meat was cooked over here on the spit above the fire," said Mrs.

Ledbetter, turning to the fireplace. Then a look of surprise came over her face. "What on earth is that suit of armor doing in here? There certainly weren't any knights in the kitchen back then!"

Ali bit her lip, praying that Barry wouldn't move. Mrs. Ledbetter stared hard at the suit of armor for a minute and then shrugged. "Someone must have moved it," she murmured to herself. "Well, anyway, class, as I was saying—"

"Hey, Ali." Genie had wiggled out of the pocket again and was tugging at Ali's sweatshirt. "I know how I can help Barry look as if he belongs in the kitchen!"

"No, Genie!" Ali whispered in alarm. "You promised you wouldn't do any magic!"

But it was too late. There was a tiny

puff of glittery smoke and suddenly Barry was wearing a blue and white striped apron over his suit of armor. He held an egg whisk in one of his metal-covered hands.

"That doesn't help at all, Genie!" Ali protested, but Genie was already wriggling back down inside the pocket.

"And it was the job of the kitchen boy to turn the spit to make sure the meat cooked properly," Mrs. Ledbetter went on. Ali held her breath as the guide turned back to the fireplace. This time Mrs. Ledbetter's eyes almost popped out of her head when she saw Barry's outfit.

"Well!" Mrs. Ledbetter said as everyone but Ali burst out laughing. "I can see that someone's been playing a *very* silly joke."

Ali thought quickly. "Weren't some knights specially trained to help in the kitchen?" she piped up. She had to stop Mrs. Ledbetter from going over to the armor or she might realize there was somebody inside!

Mrs. Ledbetter raised her eyebrows. "I've never heard of such a thing!"

"Um . . . I read it in a book somewhere," Ali babbled. She turned bright red as everyone in the class, including Mary, stared at her. "I've been doing a lot of research about castles and knights. And I've learned all about the kitchens. I'm very interested in cooking."

For the first time Mrs. Ledbetter looked a bit unsure of herself. "Well, let's move on," she said hastily. "Now

I'm going to take you to the Long Gallery!"

Ali breathed a sigh of relief as the group set off again.

"What do you mean you're interested in cooking?" Mary nudged Ali, a grin on her face. "What about those pepper cookies?"

"I had to stop Mrs. Ledbetter from going over to Barry," Ali explained.

Mary frowned. "Do you think he put on that apron and picked up that egg whisk himself? It's just the sort of silly thing he *would* do!"

"Maybe someone in our class did it as a joke," Ali said. "Come on, let's go and help him move."

"Quick, get me out of here. I feel as if I'm about to catch fire!" Barry grumbled when Ali and Mary ran over to him. Ali touched the armor. It did feel hot. Poor Barry must have felt as if he was cooking in a giant saucepan!

"And who put this stupid whisk in my hand?" Barry added crossly.

"Never mind," Ali said. "Just keep following us, okay?"

Muttering to himself, Barry clanked out of the kitchen behind Ali and Mary. The class had stopped farther down the corridor, and Mrs. Ledbetter was pointing to some of the beautiful paintings that hung on the walls. Ali began to wonder how much sand still had to run through the hourglass. The wishes might come to an end very soon, she thought hopefully, and then Barry would be able to get out of the armor.

"Genie?" Ali whispered, tapping gently on the backpack pocket. "Genie, show me the hourglass."

There was no reply. Puzzled, Ali peered into the pocket. Then she let out a gasp.

Genie had vanished.

Chapter Five
Big Trouble for Little Genie

Ali was so shocked that for a moment she couldn't think straight. Had Genie climbed out of the pocket, or had she fallen out?

Ali spun around to look back down the corridor. All of a sudden, a familiar flash of pink caught her eye. The painting on the wall beside her showed an old-fashioned ballroom. Men in black suits were waltzing around the dance floor with ladies wearing full-skirted ball gowns. And there, half hidden behind some of the other dancers, was Genie!

She was the same size as the other people in the painting but was still wearing her swirly-patterned floaty pink pants and top. A very dashing young man with a twirly mustache was whisking her around the dance floor.

"Oh no," Ali groaned. Genie had put herself into the picture!

Not wanting to draw attention to herself, Ali crept over to the painting. She *had* to talk to Genie and get her out of there right away.

"Keep away from the pictures, please!" Sharp-eyed Mrs. Ledbetter had spotted Ali. "Now if you'll all follow me, I'll take you to see a very special painting."

Ali glanced anxiously over her shoulder at the ballroom picture while Mrs. Jasmine and Mrs. Ledbetter ushered the group down the corridor. She'd have to try to give the rest of the class the slip so she could stay behind and speak to Genie.

There was a clank from behind her as a suit of armor moved away from the wall and started to shuffle across the carpet. "Come on, Ali," said Barry. "Why are you hanging around?"

"I'm coming," Ali said. She took another look at the painting and blinked. The dashing young man was dancing with a dark-haired lady in a blue dress. Genie had vanished again!

"Where can she be *now*?" Ali muttered as she helped Barry down the corridor.

"This is the most famous painting in the castle," Ali heard Mrs. Ledbetter say. The guide was standing in front of an enormous gilt frame. It was so big that it took up the whole end wall of the gallery. Ali left Barry by the wall and squeezed between the others to take a closer look.

In the foreground of the picture there was a knight brandishing a lance at a very real-looking dragon with green scales. A maiden was chained to a rock behind them, waiting for the knight to rescue her.

"It was painted by Wolfgang Popplehoff, who was a very famous artist," Mrs. Ledbetter went on.

Tiffany Andrews sniffed. "My dad's got a painting like that in his study. Ours is *much* nicer."

Mrs. Ledbetter glared at her. Ali could see that Tiffany was starting to get on her nerves! Ali smiled, but then she spotted something that knocked the smile right off her face.

The lady chained to the rock was Genie!

Ali leaned forward as far as she dared and stared hard at the picture. The maiden in distress had a blond ponytail and was wearing sparkling pink pants. It *was* Genie! She was staring up at the fire-breathing dragon, looking scared to death.

As soon as Mrs. Ledbetter turned away to take the group to the next room, Ali put her ear close to the picture.

"Help!" called a tiny voice. Genie sounded really frightened.

Ali glanced at the knight. He didn't look as if he was going to be very much help. He looked as scared as Little Genie.

Ali bit her lip. She'd promised herself she wouldn't use any wishes on this trip, but she knew there was only one thing she could do to get Genie out of trouble.

"Come on, Ali," Mary called. She was helping Barry to follow the others.

"In a sec," Ali called back. "I've got to get something out of my backpack first." She hung around, pretending to unfasten her backpack, until Mary and Barry had left the gallery. Then she turned to the picture again and took a deep breath.

"I wish I was inside the picture too," Ali said, adding quickly, "with Barry's armor to help me fight the dragon and rescue Genie!"

There was a puff of silvery smoke, and a gust of cold wind lifted Ali off her feet. Coughing, she flapped her hand in front of her face until the smoke began to clear. She was standing on the rock next to Genie. In front of them the knight was halfheartedly waving his lance at the dragon, which was roaring and spitting flames. It looked as if Ali was going to have to rescue the knight, too!

Ali looked down at herself. Something didn't feel right. Then her heart sank. She'd wished for Barry's armor . . . but instead she was wearing the striped apron and holding the egg whisk! What use would they be against an enormous fire-breathing dragon?

"Am I glad to see you!" Genie exclaimed. "It took you long enough to make the wish." She nodded in the direction of the knight, who was trying to dodge the flames the dragon was breathing at him. "I don't think *he's* going to rescue me!" Then Genie stared doubtfully at the egg whisk in Ali's hand. "But I'm not sure *you've* brought the right equipment."

"I wished for Barry's armor," Ali grumbled, helping Genie out of her chains. Luckily, they were just looped around her wrists and ankles, so it was quite easy to untangle her. "But I got the whisk and the apron instead!"

"The wish didn't work because you

wished to be in the picture *and* for Barry's armor, that's why," Genie said, rubbing her wrists. "That's two wishes, really. Well, call it one and a half."

"Never mind," Ali said urgently, hearing the dragon roaring behind them. "Do some genie magic and get us out of here!"

But before Genie could do anything, the air echoed with the sound of flapping wings. Ali felt hot, fiery breath on her neck. The dragon was flying straight toward them!

Chapter Six
Cool, Fresh Breath

"Help!" Ali cried, waving frantically at the knight. "Help!"

"Sorry," the knight said, looking petri-fied. "I'm not a real knight, you know. I'm just the kitchen boy. Baron Wolfgang asked me to pose for this picture, but I don't know anything about fighting drag-ons!" And looking very apologetic, he scrambled onto his horse and galloped off, clinging to the horse's mane. "By the way, nice whisk," he called back over his shoulder to Ali. "Very good quality."

"Yes, but it's not going to help me stop a dragon, is it?" Ali threw the whisk down in disgust.

The dragon was hovering above Ali and Genie now, shooting flames in their direction. Ali ducked, feeling the ends of her hair singe.

"Quick!" Genie said suddenly. "Get Barry's peppermints out of your backpack!"

Ali stared at her. "Genie, this is no time to be thinking about food. We're being attacked by a fire-breathing dragon!"

"Just *do* it," Genie insisted.

With shaking fingers, Ali undid the other backpack pocket and pulled out a handful of peppermints. She passed them to Genie, who waited until the dragon opened his mouth to roar again. Then she hurled the mints toward him.

A couple of them landed right in the dragon's mouth. He stopped roaring and looked surprised. There was a faint *hiss* and all the flames disappeared.

Genie turned to grin at Ali. "See? These mints give you 'cool, fresh breath'!" she

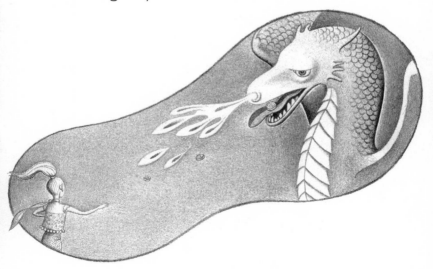

explained, singing the last few words of a jaunty tune. "I saw the commercial while you were at school."

"Thank goodness for that!" Ali said. The dragon was crunching noisily on the peppermints as if he was enjoying them. He didn't seem half so scary now. Gently flapping his wings, he flew down and landed on the rock beside them. Then he began nosing around Ali's backpack like an inquisitive dog.

"Here, have them all!" Ali said. She took out the rest of the peppermints and put them down on the rock. The dragon sniffed at them, his enormous nostrils quivering.

Genie reached out and patted his shiny green scales. "He's cute, isn't he?" she

said. "Can we take him home with us?"

Ali shook her head, remembering what had happened with the tiny purple tiger that had come to life from the chocolate ad. Although he was very cute, it had been nearly impossible to keep him a secret from Ali's mom. A fire-breathing dragon would be even more of a challenge! "I think we'd better leave the dragon here in the painting where he belongs," she said. "Come on, let's get back to the castle before anyone wonders where I've gone."

"Okay." Genie sighed, patting the dragon on the head. "Bye!"

She raised her arms in the air and murmured a couple of magic words. A cool breeze swirled around Ali and Genie, lifting them off their feet and wrapping them in drifts of smoke.

Ali closed her eyes. When she opened them again, she found to her relief that she was back in the Long Gallery beside the painting. Genie was mini size again, hanging out of Ali's backpack pocket.

"I hope the picture isn't damaged," Ali said. But the painting was exactly the same as it had been before, with the handsome kitchen-boy knight fighting the fire-breathing dragon. The only difference was that there was now a red-haired lady in a long white dress chained to the rock instead of Genie.

"Thank goodness for that!" Ali said. "Now we'd better try to find everybody. I have no idea where they've gone."

"Shhh." Genie put her finger to her lips and grinned. "If you listen carefully, you can hear Barry Jones clanking!"

Ali followed the noise of moving armor out of the Long Gallery and down another corridor. The rest of her class was heading to the castle restaurant to eat their packed lunches. By the time Ali joined them, they were already sitting at the tables in the wood-paneled room, which was hung with more paintings. Barry's suit of armor was standing in the corner, and Mary was sitting at the table closest to it.

"I'm starving!" Barry was complaining in a muffled voice.

"We'll have to share our lunches with Barry," Mary said in a low voice to Ali. "Otherwise he's not going to get anything to eat."

"Okay," Ali agreed. She opened her lunch box and took out a cheese and tomato sandwich. She made sure that no one was watching her. Tiffany Andrews and her friends were sitting at the next table. Ali knew that Tiffany would go straight to Mrs. Jasmine if she found out Barry was stuck inside a suit of armor. But Tiffany, Sara, and Melanie were too busy talking to take any notice, so Ali quickly slid the sandwich through the slit in Barry's visor.

"Cheese? Yuck!" Barry said in disgust. "I hate cheese."

"I've got ham," Mary said, pushing a sandwich through the hole.

"I hope it hasn't got any lettuce on it," Barry grumbled.

Ali and Mary rolled their eyes at each other. Then Ali's heart sank as she noticed Mrs. Ledbetter staring at the suit of armor from the other side of the room.

"That's not supposed to be in here!" Looking very put out, the guide stood up with her hands on her hips. "Who's moving all these suits of armor around, that's what I'd like to know! I'll have to have a word with the curator about this."

"Keep still, Barry," Ali whispered nervously.

"Mrs. Ledbetter, perhaps you could tell us something about the paintings in this room while we're eating our lunch," Mrs. Jasmine said.

"Very well." Mrs. Ledbetter waved her hand around the room. "These are all portraits of the Popplehoff family through the centuries."

Ali gazed at the pictures. The Popplehoffs seemed quite a miserable bunch. Not one of them was smiling.

"They don't look like much fun, do they?" Genie whispered, echoing Ali's thoughts as she poked her head out of the backpack pocket. "Can I have some lunch?"

Ali rooted around in her lunch box and gave Genie a chunk of cheese and the top of a chocolate sandwich cookie.

"This is Henrietta Popplehoff when she was ten years old." Mrs. Ledbetter pointed at the portrait hanging above the fireplace. It showed a sulking girl in a frilly

blue and white dress, holding a china doll. "Apparently, Henrietta was very spoiled," Mrs. Ledbetter explained, glancing at Tiffany Andrews. "She used to have a fit of temper if her father didn't bring her a new doll whenever he'd been away from home. The collection of dolls we saw in the Green Bedroom belonged to her."

"Henrietta sounds even brattier than Tiffany!" Mary whispered to Ali.

"I'm still starving," Barry moaned from inside the armor. "Can I have a cookie?"

Making sure no one was looking, Ali slid a chocolate cookie through the opened visor and sat down again.

"Henrietta's ghost is supposed to haunt the castle," Mrs. Ledbetter added with a smile. "Some people claim to

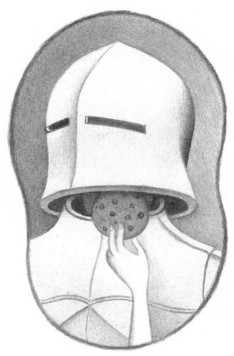

have seen a ten-year-old girl in an old-fashioned blue and white dress wandering about."

"Don't be scared, class," Mrs. Jasmine said hastily. "There's no such thing as ghosts."

"Oh, I wouldn't be scared if I saw a ghost." Tiffany Andrews yawned, looking bored. "I'd just walk right up to it and say 'Boo!'"

Sara and Melanie giggled.

"I tell you what." Tiffany had lowered her voice, but Ali and Mary could still hear what she was saying. "Let's go and look for the ghost!"

"Ooh, yes!" Sara and Melanie said together.

The three girls pushed back their chairs and slipped out of the restaurant. No one saw them go except for Ali and Mary.

"I bet Tiffany would be frightened out of her wits if she did meet a ghost," Mary said, laughing. "I wish she would!"

"So do I," Ali agreed.

Then she froze. Oh no! Had she just used her third wish? What if Tiffany really *did* meet a ghost now? *But it wasn't really my wish,* Ali told herself. It was Mary's wish—she had just agreed with it! But she couldn't stop worrying.

Mary was feeding Barry another chocolate cookie, so Ali tapped gently on the backpack pocket. "Genie, was that a wish?" she whispered.

Genie appeared, rubbing her eyes and yawning. "Was what a wish?" she asked. "Sorry, I didn't hear anything. I was having a nap."

Quickly Ali explained what she had said when she was talking to Mary.

"I don't know if that was a wish or

not," Genie said. "I do feel a bit strange, but that doesn't necessarily mean there's magic around. It might be the cheese I just ate."

Suddenly a bloodcurdling scream echoed down the corridor, and Tiffany, Sara, and Melanie rushed into the restaurant.

"It's the ghost!" Tiffany shrieked, her face white. "We've seen the ghost!"

Chapter Seven
A Spooky Problem

"Oh no!" Ali muttered guiltily. "It *was* my third wish!"

"Do you think it's really a ghost?" Mary gasped, her eyes wide with excitement.

Everyone started talking at once. Tiffany, Sara, and Melanie were shaking all over, and Tiffany was quite hysterical.

"Th-there she was in the corridor, r-right in front of our eyes," she stammered. "Penrietta Hopplehoff—

I mean, Henrietta Popplehoff. She had that very same blue and white dress on!" She pointed dramatically at the portrait above the fireplace.

"Tiffany, do try to calm down," Mrs. Jasmine said, patting her on the back.

Mrs. Ledbetter looked stern. "Henrietta's ghost is just a story we made up for the visitors," she said. "Are you girls playing a silly joke?"

"They *do* seem scared," Mrs. Jasmine pointed out.

Ali grabbed her backpack. "Let's go and look," she said to Mary.

Mary stared at her in amazement. "You're joking!" she gasped. "Aren't you frightened?"

Ali shook her head. She couldn't see

any reason to be scared of a magic ghost. "I bet there's nothing there at all," she said.

"Okay, I'll come with you," Mary said bravely. "But what about Barry?"

Ali glanced over at the suit of armor. Faint snores were coming from inside.

"He's having a nap!" she said with a grin. "Come on."

Everyone else was still crowding around Tiffany and her friends, so they didn't notice when Ali and Mary slipped out. The girls walked down the corridor and looked around, but they couldn't see anything.

"There's no one here," Mary said, sounding relieved. "It looks like Tiffany and the others were just playing a joke."

Ali felt relieved too. Perhaps she hadn't used her third wish after all.

"WHOOOOOOO!"

Ali and Mary jumped, then froze as a girl in a long blue and white dress drifted out from behind a cupboard and flew straight toward them. Her old-fashioned buttoned boots hovered a few inches above the floor, and Ali could see right through her.

"Oh!" Ali and Mary gasped together.

"It *is* Henrietta Popplehoff!" Mrs. Ledbetter shrieked behind them.

Ali and Mary spun around. They hadn't noticed the guide following them into the corridor.

"I must fetch the curator at once!" Mrs. Ledbetter said, and she dashed off.

Henrietta stopped halfway down the corridor and glared at Ali and Mary.

"What are we going to do?" Mary whispered, clutching Ali's arm.

"Don't worry," Ali said confidently. "I don't think she's going to hurt us." After all, Henrietta was only there because of her wish. Genie's magic must have used the portrait of Henrietta to come up with the ghost that Ali had wished for.

Crash!

Mary jumped again, looking scared out of her wits.

"That came from inside the restaurant," Ali said. "I think Barry's fallen over! You'd better go and help him."

"But I can't leave you here with ... with the ghost!" Mary stammered.

"I'll be fine," Ali promised, feeling a bit embarrassed that Mary thought she was being really brave. "But don't say anything to Mrs. Jasmine, or Tiffany will panic again!"

Mary nodded. Then she backed cautiously toward the restaurant door, her eyes fixed on Henrietta.

"Um—excuse me, but she's not a magic ghost!" Genie said suddenly. She had popped up out of the pocket and was staring at Henrietta.

Ali frowned. "Of course she is!" she said. "I used my third wish, I told you."

Genie shook her head. "No, you didn't. If I'd used my magic to make a ghost, it would be a nice, smiley, cheerful one, not a miserable one like that!"

Ali felt all the color drain from her face. "You mean she really *is* a ghost?"

"I suppose so," Little Genie said solemnly.

"Help!" Ali whispered, her throat suddenly dry.

"Don't worry." Genie wriggled out of the backpack and perched on Ali's shoulder. "She doesn't look that scary. She just looks sad, that's all. Don't you think we should see if we can cheer her up?"

Ali looked at Henrietta more closely. Genie was right. The ghost didn't look scary anymore. Her shoulders drooped and she was staring down at the floor.

"Hello, Henrietta," Ali said. She made herself walk toward the sad little ghost, even though her knees were shaking.

"What's the matter? Can we do anything to help?"

Henrietta looked at her. Her sulky face lit up when she spotted Genie sitting on Ali's shoulder.

"A doll!" she shrieked. "A new doll!"

Before Ali could do anything, Henrietta swooped forward, her hands out-stretched. She grabbed Little Genie and flew right up into the air, out of Ali's reach.

Chapter Eight
The Third Wish

"Help!" Genie yelled. "Ali, help me!"

Ali watched in dismay as Henrietta floated up to the ceiling. She landed on the crystal chandelier and set all the glass beads tinkling. Then she began to examine Genie more closely. She patted and stroked her hair and felt her clothes.

"Stop it!" Genie wailed. "I'm *not* a doll!" She stared down at Ali and then covered her eyes with her hands. "Get me down, Ali!" she called. "You know I don't like heights!"

"A talking, moving doll!" Henrietta's eyes opened wide in delight. "I've never had one of those before."

"Henrietta!" Ali called urgently. "You have to let Genie go. She's not—"

Ali stopped. She had been about to tell Henrietta that Genie was not a doll at all, but she wasn't sure Henrietta would understand. After all, Genie was the same size as a doll, and Ali was pretty certain that Henrietta had never come across a real, live genie before.

And Ali wasn't supposed to tell *anyone* about Little Genie. If she did, Genie could be sent back to live in her Lava lamp.

"Please give Genie back to me, Henrietta," Ali said. "She's my doll, not yours."

Henrietta scowled at Ali, while Genie looked outraged.

"Excuse me!" Genie protested. "I'm *not* a doll, I'm a—"

"Shhh!" Ali said quickly. She glanced at Henrietta. She had turned Genie upside down and was examining her curly-toed pink shoes. "We can't tell her the truth. It might scare her."

"Scare her!" Genie repeated, hanging upside down with her ponytail swinging wildly. "She's a ghost!"

"I know, but ghosts might get scared too," Ali pointed out. "Can't you use your magic to escape?"

"It won't work on a ghost," Genie replied.

"Henrietta," Ali called more loudly. "Please give Genie back to me."

"No!" Henrietta retorted triumphantly.

"You can't have her back. She's my doll now."

As she spoke, she flew off the chandelier and floated toward the stairs. Ali hurried after her. Henrietta flew up the stairs and along the corridor. Panting, Ali reached the landing just in time to see the ghost disappear into the Green Bedroom with Little Genie still clutched in her hand.

Ali ran down the corridor and stopped in the doorway. Henrietta was sitting on top of a glass case pointing to the dolls inside.

"This one in the blue satin dress is my favorite," she was saying to Genie.

"Genie?" Ali moved cautiously into the room. "Are you okay?"

"I'm fine, I think," Genie said, still looking a bit nervous. "Henrietta's telling me all about her dolls."

"They're really beautiful," Ali said loudly, walking farther into the room. She wondered if there was a chance she could grab Genie. Henrietta didn't seem to be taking much notice of her at the moment. She was too busy looking at the dolls in the glass case.

"If you've got all these lovely dolls," Ali went on, "why do you want Genie?"

Henrietta turned and glared at Ali. "I haven't got any dolls anymore," she snapped. "That's why I need a new one." She clutched Little Genie to her even more tightly. Genie gave a muffled squeak.

"I thought all these dolls were yours," Ali said, pointing at the glass cases.

"Yes, but I can't have them." Henrietta looked sad. "They're locked away. I miss them."

Ali found herself feeling quite sorry for the forlorn little ghost. "Why can't you just play with them at night when no one's here, and then put them back in the morning?" she suggested.

Henrietta looked scornfully at her. "I'm a ghost, silly," she said. "I can't open the glass cases."

Ali frowned. "I thought ghosts could walk through walls and stuff like that," she said. "Can't you just get through the glass?"

Henrietta's ghostly cheeks turned a

very pale shade of pink. "I'm not very good at walking through walls," she confessed. "I missed a lot of classes at Spook School."

"Mmm," Ali said, glancing at Genie. "That reminds me of someone else!"

"There must be a way we can help Henrietta play with her dolls again," Genie whispered to Ali. "Then she'll let me go."

"Maybe I could get the dolls out of the glass case," Ali said.

"I don't think that's a good idea," said Genie. "Look." She pointed to a sign on the wall that read THESE DISPLAY CASES ARE PROTECTED BY ALARMS.

"Anyway, we can't just let Henrietta take the dolls," Genie added. "People will notice they're gone and call the police."

"What Henrietta needs is some *new* dolls," Ali said.

"Well, you still have one wish left," Genie reminded her in a low voice. "Wishing for Tiffany to see a ghost wasn't a real wish, remember?"

"Oh yes!" Ali started to feel more hopeful. "Henrietta, if I give you some brand-new dolls, will you give Genie back to me?"

Henrietta looked amazed. "New dolls?" she repeated. "For me?"

"Lots of them," Ali told her.

Henrietta nodded eagerly. "Oh yes," she said. "I don't want this old doll if I can have lots of new ones."

"Thanks a lot!" Genie muttered.

Ali took a deep breath. "I wish . . . ," she began in a low voice, so that Henrietta couldn't hear her. ". . . I wish that Henrietta had lots and lots of brand-new dolls, all for herself!"

Chapter Nine
Hunt for the Dolls

Ali smiled encouragingly at the ghost while she waited for the familiar puff of pink smoke. She just hoped Genie was clever enough to make the dolls appear under the bed or in the wardrobe or something. Henrietta might get scared if she saw dolls appear out of thin air!

But there wasn't even the usual puff of smoke. Genie had been *very* clever, Ali thought, feeling impressed.

Henrietta was frowning at Ali. "Where are they?" she demanded.

"Yes, Genie." Ali winked at Genie. "Where are they?"

Genie shrugged. "I don't know," she said.

"What do you mean, you don't know?" Ali said worriedly.

"Where are my dolls?" Henrietta demanded in a sharp voice. "If you don't give me my new dolls, you're not getting Genie back!"

"Think, Genie!" Ali urged. "Where could they be?"

Genie pulled thoughtfully at her ponytail. "Well . . . ," she began. "I suppose they could have appeared wherever Henrietta used to keep her dolls before."

Ali turned to Henrietta. "Where did you keep your dolls?"

"In my bedroom," Henrietta replied in a sulky voice. "I had a special cupboard where I put them all."

"Wasn't this your bedroom?"

"No!" Henrietta said, looking offended. "My room is much nicer than this."

"Can you take us there?" Ali asked.

Henrietta looked suspiciously at Ali for a moment. Then she nodded. Still clutching Genie, she flew off the glass case and over Ali's head toward the door.

Ali followed her. She hoped that the dolls were in Henrietta's old bedroom. If they weren't, they could be *anywhere* in the castle. Ali glanced at her watch. She didn't have much time to go on a hunt for dolls. Her class would be leaving soon.

Henrietta led the way along the corridor while Ali jogged behind her. Luckily no one else was around. Halfway down the corridor they came to a narrow spiral staircase, which was roped off. A sign on the wall read CLOSED TO THE PUBLIC. DANGER! KEEP OUT.

Ali stopped. "Is it safe?" she asked nervously.

Henrietta nodded. "They're just doing some redecorating," she said. "They're always doing stuff like that. But it never looks as nice as when *I* lived here. Come on."

She flew up the staircase. Ali ducked under the rope and followed her, checking first to make sure no one was watching. At the top of the stairs, she reached a beautiful bedroom. There was a four-poster bed with pink silk curtains, and lots of cupboards. Two big wooden toy boxes stood in the middle of the floor, and several old-fashioned toys lay beside them.

"They left all my other toys here," Henrietta said with a sigh. "But I miss my dolls."

"Where did you keep them?" Genie asked, sounding as if she was being squeezed rather uncomfortably under Henrietta's arm.

"In that armoire over there." Henrietta pointed across the room at a tall, wide wardrobe. A stepladder and some tins of paint stood beside it, where the castle workmen had been repainting the ceiling.

"Let's have a look inside," Ali said, wondering what they would do if there were no dolls in the armoire.

Henrietta flew across the room. "I used to have so many dolls," she said sadly. She looked at Ali. "You'll have to open the doors."

Ali took a deep breath and flung open the doors while Henrietta and Genie peered curiously over her shoulder.

"Oh!" Henrietta gasped.

The armoire was lined with shelves. And to Ali's relief, each shelf was crammed with dolls!

"Wow!" Ali breathed. "There are tons of them!"

Then she looked at them more closely, and her heart sank right down to her toes. These weren't expensive china dolls dressed in old-fashioned silk and satin clothes. They were all dressed like Genie! Or more precisely, they were dressed like Ali's gran, in the photos Ali had seen of her from the sixties. Some of the dolls were wearing bright green and pink miniskirts, while others wore silver coats and silver knee-high boots.

"Groovy, aren't they?" Genie said proudly. "That's what all the cool chicks are wearing these days."

Ali groaned. What would Henrietta think?

For a moment or two, Henrietta seemed too amazed to say anything.

"Do you like them?" Ali asked.

"I *love* them!" Henrietta replied. She clapped in delight, forgetting all about Genie, who fell to the floor with a yelp. Ali dashed forward and caught her just before she hit the carpet.

"The clothes are lovely," Henrietta cooed, picking up one of the dolls and smoothing down her silver miniskirt.

Genie gave Ali a thumbs-up.

"I can remember when people who wore clothes just like this visited the castle," Henrietta went on. "I can't wait to play with them!"

"Well, have fun," Ali said, glancing at her watch again. "I'm afraid we've got to go now. Goodbye, Henrietta."

Genie looked disappointed. "Can't we stay for a minute?" she asked. "I want to check out some of those outfits. Do you think that silver miniskirt would fit me?"

"Never mind the clothes," Ali whispered. "We'd better get out of here before Henrietta changes her mind and wants you back." She popped Little Genie into the backpack pocket. "Enjoy your new dolls," she said to the ghost.

Henrietta didn't reply. She was taking more dolls out of the cupboard.

"Phew!" Ali closed the bedroom door behind her. "That was close, Genie. I thought she was never going to let you go."

"You and me both!" Genie replied as Ali hurried down the narrow staircase. "But you do know that all the dolls are going to disappear when the sand runs through the hourglass, don't you?"

Chapter Ten
Ghostly Gifts

Ali's mouth fell open. She'd forgotten about that. "How much time is left?" she asked anxiously.

Genie held up her wrist. To Ali's dismay, there were only a few grains of sand left to trickle through.

"Poor Henrietta," Genie said. "She's going to be really sad when the dolls disappear."

Ali felt very sorry for Henrietta too.

And even more troubling was that if the dolls disappeared before Ali and her class left the castle, Henrietta might come after her and try to get Genie back! *Maybe I can get her some more dolls from somewhere?* Ali wondered as she ran down the main staircase. *I know! The gift shop might have some!*

"Ali!"

Ali jumped. Mary was waving at her from the other end of the corridor.

"Where have you been?" she asked. "I've been looking for you everywhere. You missed seeing the dungeons and the Great Hall."

"I followed the ghost upstairs, and then I couldn't find you again," Ali explained.

"Oh, yes, the ghost!" Mary lowered her

voice. "What happened? No one knows whether to believe Tiffany. And now Mrs. Ledbetter's saying she saw it too!"

"I think it was a real ghost," Ali said cautiously. "But I don't suppose we'll see her again." At least, she hoped they wouldn't!

"Wow!" Mary breathed. "A real ghost! Wait till I tell Daniel!" Daniel was Mary's thirteen-year-old brother.

"Has Mrs. Jasmine noticed I've been missing?" Ali asked.

"She wondered where you were, but I told her you'd stopped to sketch some things," Mary said.

"Thanks," Ali said. Suddenly she realized that there was no suit of armor standing nearby. "Where's Barry?"

Mary grinned. "He finished off both our lunches and then said he wanted another nap, so I left him in the restaurant." She stared anxiously at Ali. "But I don't know what we're going to do if he doesn't get out of the armor before we have to go home."

"He'll find a way out," Ali said, sounding a lot more confident than she felt. Although there were only a few grains of sand left to run through the hourglass, on genie time that might still take ages! They would just have to wait and see.

"Mrs. Ledbetter!" A tall, cross-looking man with glasses and a bushy beard suddenly strode past Ali and Mary. Ali noticed he was wearing a badge that said MR. MARSH, CURATOR OF POPPLEHOFF CASTLE.

"Mrs. Ledbetter," he called again. "Can I have a word with you, please?"

Ali and Mary stepped out of the way as Mrs. Ledbetter came into the corridor.

"Well, Mrs. Ledbetter," said Mr. Marsh severely, peering over the top of his glasses. "I have looked into your claim that you saw the ghost of Henrietta Popplehoff, and I have to say that I find it all very strange indeed."

"But—but I *did* see her," Mrs. Ledbetter spluttered.

"Yes, well, when I arrived at the spot where you told me you saw her, no one was there," Mr. Marsh pointed out.

"But I wasn't the only person who saw her," Mrs. Ledbetter protested. "And what about that suit of armor that keeps on moving about?"

"That's another thing." Mr. Marsh fixed Mrs. Ledbetter with a stern eye. "*I* haven't noticed any suits of armor moving around the castle. I think it's time you took a short holiday, Mrs. Ledbetter. A rest might do you good." He ushered her down the corridor.

"Poor Mrs. Ledbetter," Mary whispered to Ali. "Between Barry and the ghost, she's had a busy day!"

"But we really *did* see a ghost!"

Ali glanced around to see Tiffany Andrews looking very red in the face, arguing with Mrs. Jasmine.

"I think we've heard enough about ghosts for one day, Tiffany," Mrs. Jasmine said firmly.

"Mrs. Ledbetter saw it too," Tiffany argued, but Mrs. Jasmine ignored her and turned to the rest of the class.

"There's time for a visit to the gift shop before we get on the bus," the teacher announced. "Is everyone here?" She spotted Ali. "Oh, there you are, Ali. Did you finish all your sketches?"

Ali nodded. "Yes, Mrs. Jasmine."

"Good." Mrs. Jasmine smiled. "I'll look forward to seeing them in your project when we get back to school."

Ali gulped. She hadn't had time to take many notes or do many sketches at all. She'd have to do everything from memory!

Just then Mrs. Ledbetter came back, looking quite sheepish. Mary nudged Ali.

"Mr. Marsh must have given her quite a talking-to!" she murmured.

"This way to the gift shop," Mrs. Ledbetter said, leading the class out of the room. Ali felt a bit sorry for her, but really, it was probably best that Henrietta be left alone to play with her dolls. If everyone believed in the ghost, Henrietta would never have any peace and quiet.

The dolls! That reminded Ali that the dolls she had wished for were going to vanish, possibly quite soon. As the class filed into the gift shop, she looked around anxiously. There were all sorts of things on sale. Postcards, dish towels, toy swords, and lots of boxes of fudge, all with pictures of Popplehoff Castle on them.

Then Ali spotted something much

more useful. Piled up on a table at the other end of the room were boxes and boxes of dolls, all based on the painting of the knight and the dragon they'd seen in the Long Gallery. There were three dolls to collect—a knight in silver armor, a lady in a flowing white dress, and a scaly green dragon.

Ali counted out her money. She had just enough to pay for one of each—and a plastic sword for Jake.

"Look, Genie," Ali whispered, showing her the dolls after she had paid for them. "Do you think Henrietta will like them?"

"She'll love them!" Genie said enthusiastically. "You'd better hurry, though. All the sand has nearly run through the hourglass."

"Five more minutes, class," Mrs. Jasmine called.

Ali slipped out of the gift shop and headed upstairs. Once again she ducked under the rope that blocked off the staircase leading to Henrietta's room and dashed up the stairs. By the time she got to the top, she was out of breath and very hot.

Inside the bedroom, Henrietta had emptied the cupboard and was sitting on the floor surrounded by dolls.

"More dolls!" she said delightedly as Ali sprinted in and presented her with the dolls from the gift shop. "They're just like the painting in the Long Gallery."

"That's right," Ali puffed, running back to the door. It was a shame Henrietta couldn't keep the other dolls, but at least she'd have something to play with when the sand ran out and they all disappeared. "Bye, Henrietta."

Ali hurried downstairs again. Now she had to decide what to do about Barry. They couldn't leave him here, trapped in the suit of armor. She'd wait until the very last minute, and then, if he was still stuck and the wishes hadn't worn off, she'd just have to tell Mrs. Jasmine—

"Oh!"

Ali had rounded the corner at the bottom of the staircase and bumped straight into someone.

She gasped. "Barry!"

Barry blinked at her. There was no sign of the armor. He was yawning and rubbing his eyes. "Where is everyone?" he asked. "I had this really weird dream that I was stuck inside a suit of armor. When I woke up, I was lying on the floor in the restaurant."

Ali smiled. The sand must have run through the hourglass, the wishes were over. "Come on, we're going home now," she said, grabbing Barry's arm.

Mrs. Jasmine was gathering everyone together in the Great Hall. "Where have Ali and Barry gone to this time?" she exclaimed. "I've hardly seen them all day."

"Here we are," Ali called.

"You two must have worked very hard today," said Mrs. Jasmine. "Even you, Barry. Every time I looked for you, Mary told me you were busy somewhere else with your sketches and notes."

Barry looked puzzled. "What sketches and notes? I haven't done any!"

Ali nudged him in the ribs. "Shhh!" she whispered.

Still looking puzzled, Barry ambled off to join his friends while Mary came over to Ali.

"How did he get out of the suit of armor?" Mary demanded in a low voice.

Ali thought quickly. "I think he found some kind of catch in there to open it up," she said.

"Thank goodness for that," said Mary. "I was beginning to think we'd have to take him back in the luggage compart-ment!"

"It's not fair," Tiffany Andrews moaned

as Mrs. Jasmine shepherded the class out of the castle and toward the bus. "We *did* see a ghost!"

"Be quiet, Tiffany," said Mrs. Jasmine. "I think you, Sara, and Melanie had better sit at the front with me on the way home so that I can keep an eye on you."

Looking very glum, Tiffany and her friends did as they were told. Meanwhile, Ali and Mary managed to get two seats at the very back.

"Did you enjoy the day, class?" Mrs. Jasmine asked as the driver started the engine.

"Yes, Mrs. Jasmine," everyone chorused, except for Tiffany and her friends.

Ali joined in. She couldn't help feeling surprised when she realized that she really *had* enjoyed the day, in spite of all the genie magic. She bent over to put her backpack on the floor and Little Genie poked her head out, grinning from ear to ear.

"See?" Genie said proudly. "I told you we wouldn't get into any trouble today!"

About the Author

Miranda Jones lives in a regular house in London. She's sure a genie bottle would be much more exciting.

Collect all of the Little Genie Books!

How much magic can one little genie make?

Little Genie

MIRANDA JONES
illustrated by David Galver

Is it a good idea to let a little genie pretend
to be a human girl?

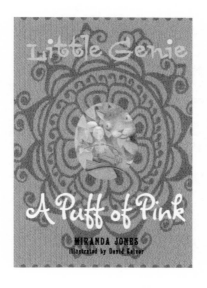

Will Ali have to think pink forever?